Cobalt Blue

Indigo Blue

Lavender Blue

Ultramarine Blue

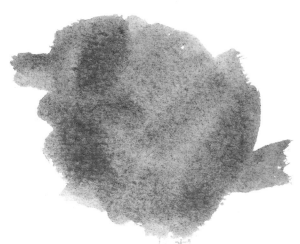

Indanthrene Blue

Cyan Blue

Prussian Blue

Manganese Blue

Midnight Blue

For Max
Love, Mommy
xoxox

Color for Rosalie.
Music for Jean-Luc.
J.-F. D.

Translated from the French by Michel Bourque

Library of Congress Cataloging-in-Publication Data Available

10 9 8 7 6 5 4 3

Published by Sterling Publishing Co., Inc.
387 Park Avenue South, New York, NY 10016
© Père Castor, Editions Flammarion, 2003
Translated from the original French UN BLEU SI BLEU
English translation copyright © 2005 by Sterling Publishing Co., Inc.
Distributed in Canada by Sterling Publishing
C/o Canadian Manda Group, 165 Dufferin Street
Toronto, Ontario, Canada M6K 3H6
Distributed in the United Kingdom by GMC Distribution Services,
Castle Place, 166 High Street, Lewes, East Sussex, England BN7 1XU
Distributed in Australia by Capricorn Link (Australia) Pty. Ltd.
P.O. Box 704, Windsor, NSW 2756, Australia

Sterling ISBN-13: 978-1-4027-2139-7
ISBN-10: 1-4027-2139-0

For information about custom editions, special sales, premium and
corporate purchases, please contact Sterling Special Sales
Department at 800-805-5489 or specialsales@sterlingpub.com

JEAN-FRANÇOIS DUMONT

A BLUE SO BLUE

Sterling Publishing Co., Inc.
New York

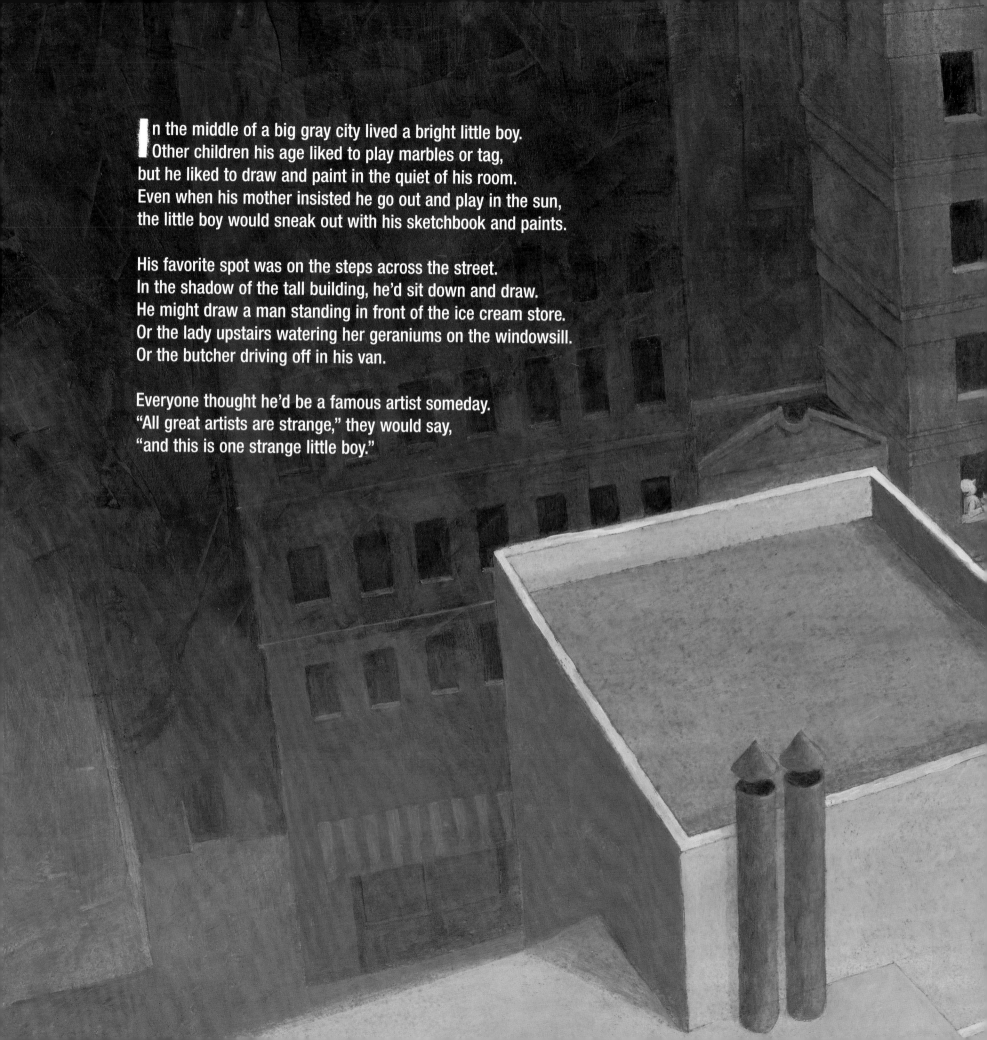

In the middle of a big gray city lived a bright little boy.
Other children his age liked to play marbles or tag,
but he liked to draw and paint in the quiet of his room.
Even when his mother insisted he go out and play in the sun,
the little boy would sneak out with his sketchbook and paints.

His favorite spot was on the steps across the street.
In the shadow of the tall building, he'd sit down and draw.
He might draw a man standing in front of the ice cream store.
Or the lady upstairs watering her geraniums on the windowsill.
Or the butcher driving off in his van.

Everyone thought he'd be a famous artist someday.
"All great artists are strange," they would say,
"and this is one strange little boy."

The little boy started having peculiar but wonderful dreams.
Night after night he kept dreaming of blue.
A blue so blue, it was both dark and bright.
A blue so blue, it was always just right.

When the little boy opened his eyes one morning,
he could still feel the blue of his dreams!
Was it cobalt blue? Was it indigo blue?
Or that hard-to-pronounce cerulean blue?

He jumped out of bed and looked through his paints.
He dipped his brush in every single blue he had.
Then he painted tiny blue spots in his book.
The little boy sighed. Not one blue was the right blue.
Not one blue was the blue of his dreams.

The little boy grabbed his book and paintbrush and ran out to the street as fast as he could.
He caught the number 7 and got off the bus in front of the art museum.

The portrait of a smiling woman first caught his eye.
He dipped his brush on her beautiful blue dress.
Then he painted a tiny blue spot in his book.
But it wasn't the right blue.

He dipped his brush in the corner of a sky.
He dipped his brush on a king's blue sash.
Then he painted tiny blue spots in his book. The little boy sighed.
Not one blue was the right blue. Not one blue was the blue of his dreams.

An old museum guard noticed the sad little boy.
He walked over to him and sat on the bench.

"What were you looking for in all those paintings?" the old guard asked.
"Why were you touching them with the tip of your brush?"

"Night after night I've been dreaming of blue," the little boy said.
"A blue so blue, it's both common and rare. A blue so blue, it's beyond compare.
Can you help me find the blue of my dreams?"

"I never traveled much," said the old guard, scratching his chin,
"but I've learned a thing or two just sitting right here.
One day I heard someone talking about the Big Blue Sea.
Perhaps *that's* the blue of your dreams."

The little boy rushed to the train station, bought a ticket, and boarded the westward train.
The train rolled all night long. It cut across the tall mountains that circled the city.
Then it zoomed through the sun-bleached prairies.

Early the next morning, the train came to a stop. The sandy beach was now in full view.
The passengers couldn't wait to get off the train to enjoy the sun.
But the little boy had only one thing in mind, so he slipped
through the crowd and ran straight to the sea.

As soon as he reached the shore, he dipped his brush
in a little blue wave that was tickling his knees.
Then he painted a tiny blue spot in his book.
The little boy sighed. It wasn't the right blue.
It wasn't the blue of his dreams.

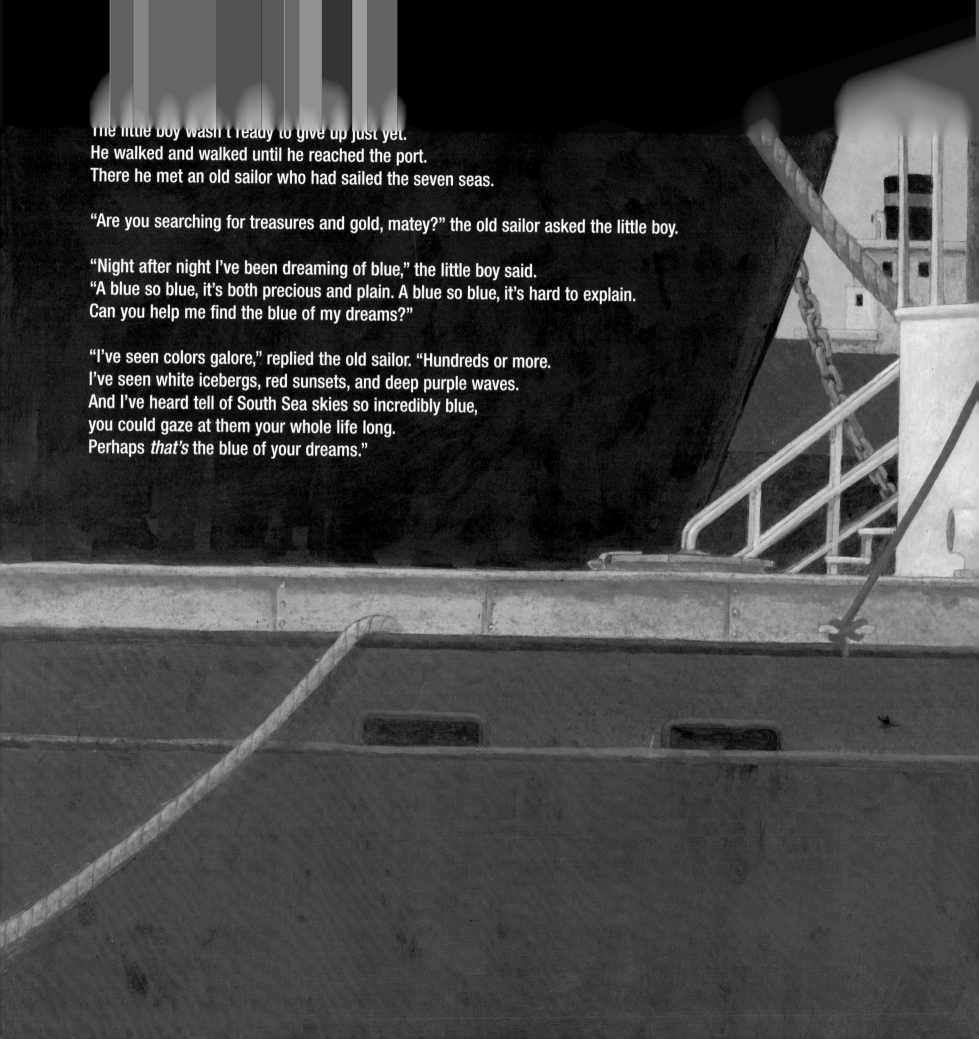

The little boy wasn't ready to give up just yet.
He walked and walked until he reached the port.
There he met an old sailor who had sailed the seven seas.

"Are you searching for treasures and gold, matey?" the old sailor asked the little boy.

"Night after night I've been dreaming of blue," the little boy said.
"A blue so blue, it's both precious and plain. A blue so blue, it's hard to explain.
Can you help me find the blue of my dreams?"

"I've seen colors galore," replied the old sailor. "Hundreds or more.
I've seen white icebergs, red sunsets, and deep purple waves.
And I've heard tell of South Sea skies so incredibly blue,
you could gaze at them your whole life long.
Perhaps *that's* the blue of your dreams."

The little boy wasted no time and boarded
the first cargo ship heading off to sea.
He braved storms and blizzards and a typhoon or two.
Then one day he landed on a tropical island.

The little boy climbed the tallest palm tree.
He dipped his brush in the rich blue sky.
Then he painted a tiny blue spot in his book. He sighed.
It wasn't the right blue. It wasn't the blue of his dreams.

The little boy sat at the foot of the tree. All his hopes were gone.
Suddenly a great big turtle came out of the sea.
"Why are you so sad?" she asked gently.

"Night after night I've been dreaming of blue," the little boy said.
"A blue so blue, it's both warm and cool. A blue so blue, it shines like a jewel.
Can you help me find the blue of my dreams?"

"I've lived many years and I've seen
all the blues you could ever imagine," said the turtle.
"Far away in America, there is something called
the blues that will even sing to your soul.
It'll make you happy. It'll make you sad.
Perhaps *that's* the blue of your dreams."

Then the turtle slipped back into the sea.

The little boy sailed across the ocean and up the Mississippi.
Sweet music was coming from an old club nearby.
He stepped inside and saw a man playing a blues song.

The little boy sat at the edge of the stage and closed his eyes.
Blues, the turtle had said, would make him happy and sad.

He stood up and dipped his brush in a string of blue notes.
Then he painted tiny blue spots in his book.
The little boy sighed. It wasn't the right blue.
It wasn't the blue of his dreams.

The little boy listened to the blues all night long, long after everyone had gone.
"Is my music making you sad?" the bluesman asked.

"Night after night I've been dreaming of blue," the little boy said.
"A blue so blue, it's both happy and sad. A blue so blue, through good and through bad.
Can you help me find the blue of my dreams?"

The bluesman rested his guitar and dropped his head.
"Long before my ancestors ever became slaves, they lived in Africa far, far away.
There, brave Blue Men roam free in the desert in their long blue robes and veils.
Perhaps *that's* the blue of your dreams."

The little boy thanked the bluesman and went on his way.
He crossed the ocean still one more time and landed on the African coast.
After roaming the desert for days and days, he met a tribe of Blue Men.

The chief looked down and smiled.
The little boy dipped his brush in the man's blue turban.
Then he painted a tiny blue spot in his book. He sighed.
It wasn't the right blue. It wasn't the blue of his dreams.

"What you are looking for I do not know," said the chief.
"Yet I do know that it may never have been very far away."

The little boy thought of his mother back home.
How he longed to see her again and be held in her arms.
He thanked the Blue Man and continued his journey.

Late one night, the little boy reached the big gray city.
A soft light was glowing in a window upstairs.
He ran up as fast as he could and opened the door.
He stopped in the doorway and saw a pair of perfect blue eyes.
Then he ran to his mother and into her arms.

The little boy noticed a tear rolling down his mother's cheek.
He dipped his brush on the edge of the tear.
Then he painted a tiny blue spot at the end of his book.
The little boy sighed.

"Night after night I've been dreaming of blue,"
he whispered to his mother.
"A blue so blue, it's both tender and strong.
A blue so blue, it felt close all along.
I looked and I asked and I started to roam,
till I found it at last—right here at home."

Scheveningen Blue

Light Turquoise
Blue

Charron Blue

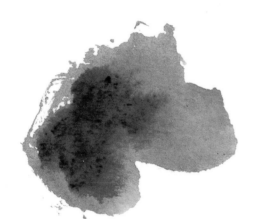

Phthalo Blue

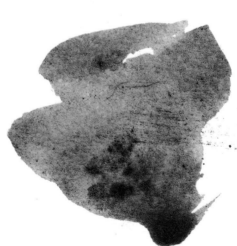

Old Holland
Blue

Dark Turquoise
Blue

Cerulean Blue

Sky Blue

Glacier Blue